When We Fly

JESS McGEACHIN

PHILOMEL

Lucy had always been good at fixing things—the wonky mailbox, broken watches, even Dad's old binoculars.

Dad needed a bit of extra help—
it was just the two of them, after all.

So when Lucy found a tiny bird who couldn't fly, behind the old garden shed, she was sure she could fix him too.

He was just a common sparrow, but Lucy didn't think he was common at all.

Lucy called him Flap.
She made a shoebox bed
while Dad took a closer look.

"I think Flap's wing is broken,"
Dad told Lucy softly.
"He won't be able to fly again."

Lucy noticed that Flap looked sad.
It's not fair, she thought.
All the other birds can still soar in the air. Why shouldn't Flap?

Surely there was a way she could help.

Lucy took her very best chalk and began to draw.
She was surrounded by a sea of crumpled paper
before she had the perfect plan.

She would need to borrow a few things.

Dad wouldn't mind—
he liked everything
Lucy made.

Keep out!
(Secret plan)

Lucy hammered, nailed,
sawed, and sewed.

It took the whole weekend,
and a few afternoons . . .

. . . but it was worth it.

Lucy placed Flap safely in the back seat and
pushed the plane to the big field behind her
house. The wheels bent the grass as she rolled
it into position.

She released the brake,
and they hurtled down the hill.

Faster and faster and faster until . . .

. . . they were flying!

They soared above fields and forests.
Flap chirped happily, and Lucy knew he
could feel the wind in his feathers again.

Lucy was so busy checking on
Flap that she didn't notice something
was wrong with the plane.

But she did notice when the wings buckled,
the rivets popped, and the propeller started to slow.

Just as the plane began to fall,
Lucy caught a glint of color from above.

Flap gave a small chirp.

There were herons and hornbills, eagles and egrets.

Every type of bird Lucy could imagine filled the sky, and they'd all come to help.

They gently lowered the plane
to a field below, where it fell
apart into a dozen pieces.

Lucy's heart sank—she'd never
be able to fix this, and now Flap
would never fly again.

Dad came and sat next to her in the grass.
Lucy told him her plan, and how everything
had gone wrong.

"Not everything that's broken can be fixed, Lucy.
But you tried to help, and Flap knows it—
that's the most important part."

Lucy fixed Flap's box so it was even better than before. He stayed with them for the last few days of summer.

But then he was gone.

Lucy and Dad loved spending time together.
Sometimes they fixed things and sometimes
they just watched the birds in the garden.

Lucy often missed Flap, but then
she remembered she had Dad.

It was just the two of them, after all.
And that was more than okay.

Flap

Hummingbird

Sedge wren

Northern cardinal

Swallow

Eurasian magpie

Splendid
fairy wren

American
goldfinch

Gouldian finch

Toucan

Lilac-breasted roller

Galah

Eastern
rosella

Flamingo

Great blue heron

Puffin

Curlew

For Caroline, who helped this book fly.

The author would like to thank Alice Sutherland-Hawes at Madeleine Milburn
Literary Agency and Michelle Madden at Penguin Random House.

PHILOMEL BOOKS

An imprint of Penguin Random House LLC, New York

First published in the United States of America by Philomel, an imprint of Penguin Random House LLC, 2021.

First published in Australia by Puffin Books, an imprint of Penguin Random House Australia Pty Ltd, 2019.

Visit us online at penguinrandomhouse.com

Library of Congress Cataloging-in-Publication Data is available.

ISBN 9780593203583

Manufactured in China

1 3 5 7 9 10 8 6 4 2

US edition edited by Liza Kaplan.
US edition designed by Lori Thorn.
Text set in Sabon.